Written Hearts

Tonya Christine Hewitt

Written Hearts

Copyright © October 2020

by Tonya Christine Hewitt

Print ISBN-13: 9798687392440

Cover Art by alkir_dep from www. depositphotos.com
Other Artists from pixabay:
Irina Kuzmina * Elina Kulish* MJ Jin * janrye
Prettysleepy *Luciana Silva* OpenClipart-Vectors
Alp Cem * Victoria_Borodinova

Published by: Tonya Christine Hewitt
Printed in the United States of America
10 9 8 7 6 5 4 3 2 1

This is loosely based on my own experiences of taking care of my mom, when she found out she had cancer. It was hard. But the one thing that was the hardest was losing her. I love my mom and so this book in a way is keeping her story alive and maybe this can help someone dealing with cancer. I have known quite a few people with the dreaded disease and it is definitely hard. My high school best friend was diagnosed with stomach cancer and sadly passed away a couple of years ago. My granddad had leukemia and I remember my mom taking care of him.

Although our friendship is platonic, I did have a penpal and friend throughout this whole ordeal and so I came up with this story. Don't get me wrong, I had lots of friends to help me go through this situation as well as the support of my loving family. My beautiful sister and her caring husband, My wonderful sister-in-law and loving brother. My supportive dad.

But it helped exchanging emails and getting out my frustrated feelings of dealing with the responsibilities of what I felt. The scars it left on my heart.

So this book is dedicated to the following:

For My Mom, I am glad we got to spend time one on one. I hate that you got sick but I loved that we were able to be in a world of our own.

For Stefan, I would have gone crazy if I didn't have your friendship when I was dealing with the hardest time in my life so thank you for that. I am glad that we met, my friend and penpal.

These two is what the book is loosely based on. Details have been fictionalized but the dealing with cancer and support I got from my penpal is very much true.

For My Aunt Louise, I just found out recently you died and that was really sad for me. I was touched when you came to my mom's funeral, even though I knew you were sick yourself.

For My Friends and Family. This is really to all of them. But I wanted to name a few that really touched me.

For Kristy, I am glad you were there for me and supported me when I read my poem to my mom at her memorial service. I never dreamed I would do the same thing at yours. I wish we could have spent more time together.

For Trisha, I'd have went nuts if I didn't have my best friend through this whole ordeal, distracting me when I needed her the most.

For Devorah, When I lost my mom, I am so glad I had you to help me get by and sending me butterflies to cheer me up.

For The Griffiths, I know Doris recently lost her husband James but I never forget how they would lovingly give us gas money so we could drive to Chattanooga so Mama could get her treatments. It meant so much to us.

For Andy and his mom, who were there for us. Same goes for Michael and his parents.

For The Shoe Dept staff who loved my mom, too.

For The Church of God at Southside whom my mom was a member, who loved my mom, too. I am glad they got to pray with her and visit. For Mike Shreve and Brother Ammons, who gave the eulogies at my mom's memorial service.

For Marlene, who experienced tragic loss herself, but who has always been a close friend of the family.

For David, who would read Psalm 103 to my mom all the time and tell her encouraging words from Brother Rick Madison.

For My Dad, who worked hard, getting my mom her Dodge Caliber that she loved.

For Elaine, who bought my mom beautiful new outfits for when she was in rehab and buying mama a memorial plaque, that said *A Beautiful Soul Lost Too Soon.*

For Deanna, who would help whenever she could with transportation needed when it came to doctor's visits and speaking for us, when we had no voice.

For Charlie, who on his birthday, dug and placed the plaque for my mom.

For Trey, Kaitlyn, and Kristyn, who helped with love, support, and cuddles.

For my Cousin Lisa, who was always a good friend to my mom.

For my Aunt Betty and her husband Norm, who would always check on my mom when she was in the hospital.

For my friend Phyllis, who happened to be my mom's high school best friend, as well as her friend Margaret.

In Memory of my loving grandparents. Two of which experienced the sadness of cancer themselves.

To the Caring nurses at Memorial, who loved my mom.

And most important is for my friend, Jesus. We couldn't have gotten through this whole ordeal if it hadn't been for you. Thank you, Jesus for loving us so.

Written
Hearts
Tonya Christine
Hewitt

Lyric

Huntley

Lyric

Dear Mr. Crisp,

    I want to thank you for writing the book, How To Deal With A Loved One Having Cancer. It touched my heart and helped me so much. I am sorry that you lost your dad last summer. I have read many books on cancer ever since my mom got diagnosed last year. I have never wrote a fan letter to an author before but your book helped me cope and I felt so connected with you and your story. Thank you for your words and that book.

Sincerely,
Lyric Sumner

Lyric

I wasn't allowed back in the chemotherapy room with my mom so I always brought my fun pack as I called it. It wasn't really that fun but I knew to bring my canvas bag every Wednesday, which was chemotherapy day. It had a Bible verse etched on the bag, reminding us that we had strength through God. Philippians 4:13 had became our theme throughout this whole ordeal.

"I can do all things through Christ
who strengthens me."
Philippians 4:13

All things, I thought silently. I didn't want my mom to be sick. But God could get me through this. Being a caregiver for a sick loved one was hard.

But I took the advice of the social worker assigned to our case. Anytime there is a sick patient, they always assign someone to each person to make sure that the caregiver or the sick person has all the resources they need. So you get a dietitian and case worker to help you through the travesty of cancer.

Cancer, the word sounds very horrid, doesn't it? I just don't understand why my mom had to get so sick and weak.

She got diagnosed in December and started radiation treatment in January. They wanted to start treatment in December but she refused, saying we deserve one happy Christmas, where no one was sick.

One of her friends had treatment before. And she said after the radiation and chemo, Louise got so weak. And my mom decided, she didn't want to get treatment, she would live with the cancer. But then, her grandkids changed her mind. She wanted to get better for them.

No, they weren't my kids. I never been married and was single. I was dating this guy named Adam Reynolds but he said I was spending too much time with my mom. Um, what a thing to say. So you see, I lost no sleep dumping him.

My brother had twin girls. Stacey and Stella and so my mom was determined to get better for the five year olds.

My dad worked all the time so that left me to be my mom's caretaker. Yes, I worked, too, but I ended up taking a leave of absence from my office job and moving in with my parents to help out with my mom.

I had a nice apartment but being with my mom was more important. I had built up a small savings account, so I was able to help out and my dad had agreed to give me two hundred dollars a month so I could help out a lot. My mom drew a little money on disability as she had a stroke years ago but thankfully, it hadn't affected her speech. I would cry if I couldn't hear my mom's sweet voice. She was partially paralyzed on her left side. I say partially because she could still get around but it took her a minute to move and her left hand trembled all the time.

But going back to what I was saying, I took the advice of the social worker assigned to our case to read some books, dealing with taking care of a loved one when they had cancer and I stumbled upon Mr. Huntley Crisp's book and for some reason felt led to write him. I knew a famous author like that would not write back because he probably didn't have time. But in my fun pack, I had packed paper and a pen to write in the meantime. I had books to read, paper to doodle and write with, and a crossword puzzle. Oh, and my Bible. My mom and I would pray a short pray all the time before she started her treatment. Wednesdays were rough on her and she felt so tired and weak by the time she did end up getting out of treatment.

I would go down to the lobby and sit and stare at the big orange fish swimming around in the aquarium. I named it Skipper as it seemed to "skip" around in the water. So while I watched the fish swim, I decided to write Mr. Crisp. I took out his book to get the address of his publisher and noticed on the back the picture of his smiling face.

The cute man with dimples stared back at me as I told him silently thank you for your book. It's just what I needed. I clutched the book to my chest as I let a tear roll down my cheek. But no, I had to be strong for my mom. I could do that, couldn't I? I just had to as I stared at the Bible verse on my bag. Mr. Crisp had been strong for his dad but the author's biography revealed his dad had passed away so he had written the book to deal with his grief. He felt led to write about their times together for he was thankful they got to spend one on one time with one another.

And so I would cherish every moment with my mom. True, I was not allowed to sit back with her in chemotherapy but we spent a lot of time together, ever since she got diagnosed. She had to take radiation Monday through Friday and then after radiation, she would go upstairs to the Chemotherapy room. The radiation treatment lasted only fifteen minutes each day but Chemotherapy dragged on for hours.

I got to know the other patients in radiation as they would sit and talk to me before they got called back. One guy had cancer of the tongue so it was hard for him to talk but he was my friend as I waved to him everyday and he would talk out of one of those voice boxes. I felt so bad for all of them. But it was amazing the amount of sad stories you heard crammed into a measly fifteen minutes.

Other caretakers would talk to me and I enjoyed the small talk as we waited patiently for our loved ones.

But chemotherapy days, I was pretty much alone for the day in the lobby. So as I waited for it to be over, I took out my pen and started to write the author I never met. I had packed a few envelopes and sealed the letter. I would mail it tomorrow.

My mom finally came down from the Chemo Floor. And I hugged her. I asked her what she wanted to do. She smiled, weakly. "I am a little hungry," she admitted.

Yay! Today was a good day, then. Sometimes, she felt too tired and weak to eat but if she was hungry that means I can take her to her favorite place to eat. So that is just what I did. It is called, "The Country Cafe." Her favorite meal is the Beef Tips Special. It comes with little roasted potatoes, her fav. I sometimes get grilled chicken but today, I opted for the same thing. Yummy. It was delicious. But now, hopefully, she could keep it down as she sipped her sprite.

After lunch, we went home and we both took long naps. All the waiting wore me out and I was relieved, she did not get sick today. But there's been times that happens. But today was a good day. I woke up before she did and kissed her forehead as she still slept. She was lightly snoring and I felt like that was the most beautiful sound in the world.

I decided while she slept I would go out to the mailbox and place it in the box. I had a few stamps on my dresser in my room so tore one off and walked to the mailbox. I put the flag up and felt a little silly I had taken the time to write to someone who probably wouldn't have time to reply back. But I went ahead and did just that.

Huntley

Dear Ms. Sumner,

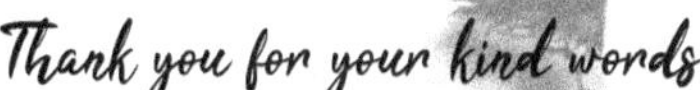

       Thank you for your kind words. It helps my book was able to reach and help someone. It was hard dealing with the death of my father so I wrote the book. When he got diagnosed with lung cancer, I thought my life was over but spending the last year with him, we had one on one time. Don't let that slip away. Memories are hard to recall but I do remember his grateful smile that I was there for him. Thank you for writing. It is always nice to hear from a fan. It may not be under the best of circumstances, you read my book, but hearing from you, I know it was worthwhile writing my book, if it even helped just one person. I am glad it was you.

Sincerely,
Huntley Crisp

Huntley

I was surprised I got a fan letter for my story about my dad. I usually get fan letters for my other books, which are fiction. But this book meant more to me than them. I had poured my heart and soul into my dad's and my story and dealing with his cancer was so very hard.

You might have heard of me. My name is Huntley Crisp and yes, I am the author of Sleuthing Sam. It is a children's book about a dog that solves mysteries. Don't get me wrong; I love being an author of such a popular series and children write me all the time, saying they love Sam. I usually write Glad you love my story and sign it, Sleuthing Sam. It makes the children feel like it's actually Sam writing them.

I always reply to every fan letter. Every four months I come up with a new mystery for Sleuthing Sam to solve. It has been compared to Scooby Doo but Sleuthing Sam finds lost pets or sniffs out bad guys. He doesn't get chased by scary ghosts or goblins. I love that I have fans and I love Sleuthing Sam. He has helped me afford my studio apartment I live in and my silver Porsche Suv.

But when Lyric wrote me, I felt so connected to her. Lyric. What an unusual name. Of course, my name was unusual, too. People are always asking me if that is my real name. Of course it is. My dad's name was Hunter and my mom's name is Lee Ann so they took both their names together and made up mine. I wondered how Lyric got hers. It sounded so musical.

Reading her mom had cancer, it hit my heart like a brick. Dealing with my dad's cancer was so hard but we had gotten really close as I became his caregiver. My mom and I are really close. She is my biggest fan of my Sleuthing Sam stories. She has all 44 books of the series.

Till I hit it big, my dad was telling me to get a real job. I was a journalist for a newspaper but he always wanted something better for me. Writing was a pointless job according to him but that all changed when I found an agent and she said I had a promising hit series. I have done book signings and promotional tours. I took time off when my dad was diagnosed. He kept on telling me he was sorry he didn't have much faith in my writing. I told him all was forgiven. I wish he had got to read my book. About us. About him.

Writing non-fiction is different than fiction. Fiction is fun but writing this non-fiction book was my heart and soul. I had not received the first fan letter about it till Lyric had written me that day.

She had written her letter on flowery stationery and mailed it in a purple envelope. I also could detect a sense of a sweet fragrance and wondered if she spritzed a little perfume on her letter.

I took out my own stationery and started penning the letter to this girl I never met but somehow had reached her with my words. I have all sorts of stationery. Being a writer, my friends and family always gave me "writing gifts." Those include pens, stationery, journals, etc. I keep them in my file cabinet, along with ideas for new stories. I decided for her letter, I would use stationery that had a nice scenery scene where it was a boat tied to the dock among the moonlit water. It gave a peaceful, serene fill.

I am also into Calligraphy and making fancy letters so sealing her letter, I wrote her address in the fancy letters I love to do. I carefully printed them on the envelope. I took out a stamp and placed it on the envelope.

I don't even know why I was bothering with this but I guess it goes back to this childhood fantasy I always had about having a penpal. Maybe that is silly and maybe Lyric would not even write back. But at least I got to try my new calligraphy pens I got for my birthday.

Huntley Crisp
250 Medlin Drive
Davenporte, FL 38512

           Lyric Sumner
           457 Lilac Rd.
           Cambridge, TN 37356

I whistled for Sam, my dog, who I had based all my detective mysteries on. He was actually an old police dog, who retired after being blind in one eye. It is actually a sad story where he jumped in front of his partner taking a bullet right in one eye. Greg Marner was forever grateful to his dog but for the dog's safety, he felt Sam should retire. And I was doing research on police dogs to inspire me for my story and I fell in love with Sam. Greg wanted to adopt him but his wife was allergic. So I got to be the proud owner of Sam. And the idea of Sleuthing Sam was born the first night Sam spent with me.

"Come on, boy, let's go to the mailbox." Sam followed me happily as I placed Lyric's letter in the box. I was almost tempted to spray some cologne on her letter since she had spritzed some perfume on hers but felt like it was over doing it.

After mailing her letter, I decided to take Sam for a walk. He loved every minute of it and I had to admit I did, too. I took him to the park and he had lots of fun, sniffing every tree and playing fetch. I have to be careful because of his eye. But Sam gets along great. After all he is the star of his own series. My publisher wanted Sam to be with me during my promotional tours but my mom watched him instead. I don't think he should be around too many crowds. Don't get me wrong. He is great with people and kids but sometimes the kids forget about being careful around his eye and so for his safety he doesn't go with me. I had a promotional tour scheduled next month so I wanted to spend time with Sam all I could since I would be so busy soon enough.

Back at home, I let my mind wander to Lyric. I hope she wrote back. Somehow, it seemed her letter brought me closer to my dad in heaven. And that is what I needed.

Lyric

Dear. Mr. Crisp,

        I did not expect to hear from you. As I had never wrote a fan letter before like I said but I didn't really expect a response. But when I received your letter, it made my day. It felt as if it deepened our connection. I wish I knew you back when your dad was sick, so we could have been there for one another. By the way, you can call me Lyric if you decide to write back, which I hope you do.

        Sincerely,
           Lyric Sumner

It absolutely floored me, Mister Huntley Crisp wrote back. I couldn't believe an actual author was writing me. Of course, I had heard of him, before I had picked up the Cancer book he had written. I had even read his Sleuthing Sam books to my nieces.

I had dabbled in writing myself. Just a few poems here and there but nothing like he had. I wondered if I should share a poem with him in my next letter but I have to wait and see if he even wrote back.

But today, I didn't have much time to think about it. Today was a bad day. My mom was very ill today. She had thrown up twice. I cleaned her up and got her into her favorite bathrobe. It was pink with butterflies. Thankfully, she managed to be alright after that. I took a dishpan and wet washcloth and dabbed her face and bathed her as she laid down on her bed. Thankfully, none had gotten her into her hair. She was just now getting gray in her black hair. She had recently turned fifty and that made me sad; she had to be sick so young. Of course, even if she was sick at a hundred, it would have been too young for me.

I asked my mom what she wanted to do after she felt a little better. "How about a movie?"

"Sure, Mom." I made sure she was okay and we decided to watch *The Trouble With Angles*. I knew she picked it for me since I loved all of Hayley Mills' films and we needed a good laugh. I snuggled up against her and we watched the movie, even though, she fell asleep on my shoulder midway through the film.

That is okay. She needed her rest. As she dozed off, I figured it would be a good time to get a little cleaning done. Before I had took a leave of absence from my job, it was just a struggle to get everything done. But I manage easier now. I clicked off the movie and went into the kitchen to attend to the dishes.

Our dishwasher is broken so as annoying as it is, I have to do them by hand. I don't mind but investing in paper plates and cutlery would be nice. I reminded myself to add it to our shopping list. I also had to remember to add Ensure. Ever since my mom started treatment, she has gotten thinner and thinner and hardly can keep anything down.

It reminded me that Huntley Crisp had said the same thing in his book about his dad, losing more and more weight, to the point he was so weak.

I hate how they say there are stages of Cancer. Stages of everything. Stages of grief. I am supposed to keep track of what my mom eats and when she gets sick, so we can go over it with her dietitian and see things we can do. I tried one of her cans of her vanilla Ensure. It tasted so bitter. I was like gross out, who can drink this stuff? But I didn't say it in front of my mom. I didn't want her to feel bad.

My mom still read in her Bible daily. She did her morning devotions. I so wondered why she had gotten sick. It made me wonder if Huntley's father had been saved before he had gotten sick. I knew by Mr. Crisp's book, that they leaned on God when they found out he got diagnosed. In his book were scriptures and bible verses throughout each chapter.

I know Christians can get sick, too. But somehow in a way, it seemed unfair anyone got sick. But I knew that it had all stemmed from Adam and Eve sinning and getting kicked out of the Garden of Eden. But all we can do is trust God and believe Jesus is Our Great Physician.

I went back to check on Mama after I washed the dishes and cleaned the kitchen. She was sleeping soundly.

I got out Huntley's letter and reread it again. Some reason, I felt so close to this stranger I never met. I had seen him on television in interviews, talking about his dog, inspiring him to do his book series. I think he mostly wrote fiction but I think I was partial to his non-fiction work. I felt as if he saw into my heart and soul, dealing with this cancer stuff.

Huntley

Dear Lyric,

Your letter made me smile. It's been awhile since I had anyone to talk to. By the way, none of this Mister Crisp stuff. It's Huntley. Let's find out more about one another. I am 36, live with my dog. He is a retired police dog actually. He is a Cocker Spaniel and blind in one eye. Usually German Shepherds or Doberman Pinchers are the most popular choice for police dogs but Sam is a great sniffer and great at finding stuff. I actually based my book series on him. You probably heard of Sleuthing Sam.

My book about my dad having cancer was the first non-fiction book I wrote and you are actually the first one who wrote me a fan letter about it. Most of the time I get letters from kids so you are older than most fans I get.

I used to work as a journalist but was able to just stay at home and write when I wrote about Sam.

My favorite color is blue, same color as my eyes and I have light brown hair. I am 6'1. Oh, I just realized you know what I look like. My picture was on the back of the book jacket. But I will enclose a picture of myself anyway. Maybe I can have one of you, too?

I hope to hear from you soon.

Your friend,

Huntley

I figured I would give Lyric an autograph picture I have of myself and Sam. It is really the only picture I have of myself. It was my agent's idea so I can give my fans a picture.

I wrote on it To Lyric, My first non-fiction fan. I am glad we met. Your new friend, Huntley.

My agent insisted I keep a stack of fifty photos at all times to give out to my fans. Leah Berkley has been my agent ever since I met her when I was journalist. I happened to be doing a feature article on an author who had her as an agent and before she found her, she had been swindled out of hundred of dollars trying to get her work published. But Leah is the real deal. The one thing you have to learn about agents, which I revealed in my article, that if an agent asks you for money right off the bat, it is dishonest. An agent relies on getting your work published to get their first paycheck. I asked Leah if she would take a look at my book about Sam and she loved it insisting it will be a series.

This was absolutely my big break. Sure, I wanted to branch out and do more books but Sleuthing Sam will always have a soft spot in my heart because of my dog and it was my first book.

And then, *How To Deal With A Loved One Having Cancer* meant a lot because of my dad. Lyric saying it meant a lot to her made my day. The dedication on the book read To My Dad, I will cherish our times together forever. Save a spot in heaven for me.

I had started writing other material but my agent said I still had to write Sleuthing Sam books but Leah called me with the most exciting news ever.

"Are you sitting down, Sam?" Leah asked.

"Yeah, what's up?" I sat down, sipping a cup of coffee. I was in a writing mood and wanted to work on new material but since I had a promotional tour coming up, Leah probably wanted to discuss the details.

"They want to make Sleuthing Sam a movie!"

"You're so kidding me!" I was flabbergasted, and did a spit take as she caught me mid-sip. I grabbed a towel that was lying nearby. I couldn't wait to tell my mom.

"It is going to be the newest cartoon movie. And we are talking big promotional items. They are making Sleuthing Sam stuffed animals. It will be coming out in December! You just have to say yes!"

"So I get to read the script right? And make sure that Sleuthing Sam stays the same?" I draw Sam myself but I wouldn't know the first thing about doing a cartoon.

"Relax; you get to approve of everything. And as far as I understand, it is combining your first three books as the movie. After your tour, you are collaborating with Brittany Blaine, who is going to adapt your words to the screenplay. It is already in the works but they just need your approval."

I talked with Leah a little more about the whole deal. I couldn't wait to tell my mom and Lyric. I realized she was at the top of the list of people I wanted to tell but I figured I would just have to wait till she wrote back.

I called Sam over to me and he came to me happily, wagging his tail. "Did you hear? You are going to be famous!" I said as I petted his soft coat. I am glad they decided to make Sleuthing Sam a cartoon. I did not want anyone else playing Sleuthing Sam but Sam and being injured he hobbled more than he used to so I didn't think they would star my dog in the film but being a cartoon, neither one of us had to feel bad.

I wonder what my dad would have said about my books becoming a movie. I knew he would tell me he was proud of me. Who knows? He was probably in heaven, saying to all his friends, "Look; that's my boy."

A smile crept on my face as I looked forward to telling my mom. And Lyric. Good things were happening lately. My tour. My book becoming a movie. And meeting Lyric. She was definitely good news on a bad day. I kinda wish I knew her when my dad was sick. I know she would have been there for me. I hoped to hear from her soon.

Lyric

Teary Eyes
The heavens cried with me
As tears poured from the sky
I heard what your test results showed
It was another hard blow
as I heard what the doctor said
echoing in my head
I did not want you to be ill
I am sick with grief;
the world stands still
But at the same time
I will hold your hand in mine
We will get through this whole ordeal
for we will follow God's will
We will get by
even as we cry

Lyric

Hi Huntley,

I figured you might want a sample of my writing. I wrote that when I first found out my mom was sick. It was a hard blow. I know you know all about it.

But I love that I have you to write too. I know we just started writing but I feel so connected to you. Is that insane?

You were asking about what I look like? Sure, I will enclose a picture but I am really just plain ole me. I am 35. I have long brown hair and hazel eyes. They change from either brown to green depending on the light and I am 5'5.

My favorite color is purple. What kind of movies do you like? My favorite movie is Summer Magic. Actually, I love all of Hayley Mills' films.

Can I ask you something? How did you get through your dad being sick? It is so hard. But at least my mom and I have one another.

My dad is always working. He is retired from the navy so my mom can afford the doctor's visits, thankfully. As for me, I used to work as a receptionist in a doctor's office but my mom being sick, I took some time off. My dad can afford to pay me to look after my mom. I only do that to make a living because I so would do that for free. But with the monthly allowance he gives me, I can afford my cellphone bill and storage locker. I used to live on my own till my mom got sick and moved back home to help out.

Just letting you know my nieces are actually going to flip when they find out I know their favorite author. Sleuthing Sam is their favorite book. They might take my picture away from me lol.

Hope to hear from you soon!
Your friend,

Lyric

Lyric

I looked at the photo Huntley sent me again. My heart did a little flutter as I stared into his blue eyes. I chided myself I was acting silly but I couldn't help it. This guy was extremely cute.

I had been really stressed with my mom and dealing with that. I didn't let my mind think of going on dates or anything like that but I had to admit sometimes I was really lonely. Talking to him helped. But I shouldn't be getting crushes on someone I barely knew. But at the same time, I felt like I knew him with each of our letters, every interview I saw on tv. But I chided myself for having silly fantasies.

I blew the photograph a kiss and hurried to my mom who was hollering for me. "Lyric, I don't feel so good."

"Oh, no, Mom. Do you need to go to the hospital?"

"I think so, sweetie." I then noticed she had threw up all over self. My poor Mom. I washed her up and changed her clothes as I threw her old ones in the washing machine. My mind flashed back to when I was sick and my mom took care of me when I was sick with gallbladder problems. I kept throwing up, even on her, and my mom said nothing as the nurse at the hospital gave her a towel to clean off as they gave me a plastic bag. I ended up having emergency surgery that night. I felt horrible but my mom made everything better. And now, I was trying to do the same for her. Dad was at work. But in case we were still at the hospital when he came home, I scribbled him a note telling him where we would be.

I held onto her as we walked to the car. She took her radiation and chemo in Chattanooga but I took her the local hospital in Cambridge.

They were actually not busy that night so they were able to take her back right away for tests. I was able to stay back in the waiting room for her and they had to hook her up with ivs and draw blood. She put on a brave face and said, "Nothing hurts as bad as when they put the nails into Jesus's hand." She said that every time she got a shot and poked and prodded with a needle. She said that she could say that to be a witness and to make herself feel better.

They wheeled her bed out of the room to take more tests. I was very worried as she had been gone for some time. I started texting on my phone to ask everyone prayer requests. I contacted Kyle, my brother, and his wife Suzy. They would have came but the twins had the chicken pox so they needed to stay with them. I knew they were tired after taking care of the cranky girls. I promised them I would keep them posted.

They finally wheeled Mama back into the room. They told me the doctor would be back to see me after awhile. "You okay, Mama?" I asked her as I kissed her cheek.

"I just feel weak." She said softly.

Just then, the doctor came back in. "You have been taking radiation for how long, Mrs. Sumner?"

"Three months," she replied. "I started in January."

"It seems that the radiation has given you colitis. We need to keep you over night to give you fluids and a blood transfusion, it seems you have lost a lot of blood. We will need for you to sign a release form."

"Is that safe? Has the blood been screened?" I asked, trying to make sure it was safe to give to my mom.

"Yes, it is completely safe but of course, there is always a percentage where anything is at risk. But if she doesn't get the blood, she will get weaker and weaker and she won't be able to survive." He said it with no emotion but with that statement, of course, we signed the papers.

"We will have to keep an eye on her, every month to make sure, she doesn't lose too much blood. So you are looking at getting a transfusion every couple of months. We will just have to make certain she doesn't lose too much blood."

We decided that I needed to go home to tell Dad after he got off work what was happening. I was going to spend the night but we needed to let him know stuff. So I spent the night texting and telling everyone what was happening. I cried and prayed as I was alone. I called my mom on her cell and we said night prayers together and she said she was okay she just wanted to sleep. I told her good night and told her I would see her in the morning.

After I hung up, I wanted to cry and scream, "Why my Mom?" But I didn't. I decided to read a chapter in my Bible. My brother had reminded me reading Psalm 103 was "the healing chapter in the Bible." So I read it and felt some better.

I decided to watch a little tv and fell asleep, worrying about my mom. Dad woke me up when I got home. "Where's Mom?"

I told him the whole story. I decided to not text him on his phone so he wouldn't worry at work and felt he needed to know in person.

In the morning, we rode together to pick up Mom. I drove since he worked basically all night. They released Mama at eleven that morning. "I feel much better." She told us. I let out air that I didn't know I had been holding with sighs of relief and thanked Jesus for taking care of her.

A nurse wheeled her to the car. I had brought a change of clothes for her to change into and so we decided we would go to Pancake Place for breakfast after my parents agreed. I knew we could not stay out too long, my dad had to get some sleep and my mom and me had the whole day. They had given her radiation treatment at the hospital instead so we had the whole day together.

When we got home, we all took naps and when we woke up, I was glad to see my mom was feeling much better.

I said a silent prayer to thank Jesus for healing my mom and asked my mom if she wanted to go shopping for a new dress. She agreed as long as I got one, too. I decided to treat her and me to the beauty salon. We did the works; our hair, manicure and a pedicure. She had been sad her hair was getting thinner from the chemo but she was glad that none had fell out. I got her some Panteen shampoo to help with it but she felt much better from our beauty day.

She couldn't wait to show Dad and I realized I wanted to take a picture and show Huntley. I hadn't mailed my letter yet so I asked Mom if she wanted to take pictures together. I had taken her to the mall and we sat together in a photo booth. I insisted we do it together and then separately. I said Dad would want a pic of just her and I could send a pic to Huntley. She knew all about me writing him. She had read a few passages of his book and was deeply moved by it as well.

We had changed into our clothes we just bought. I had bought a purple dress that was like a front wrap dress and showed my figure quite nicely. My hair hung loose in curls upon my shoulders. Mom's dress had a pink jacket on it over a pink and purple flowery dress. Ever since her stroke, she had trouble lifting her arm but I helped her get changed into the outfit. We both got new sandals as well. Mine were purple with little hearts while my mom's were pink with flowers.

I told her they could be our Easter outfits but it never hurt getting dressed up a little early. I could tell she had a full day and was a little tired so we headed home. "Thank you, Lyric, for the most perfect day. I love that we get to spend time together."

"Me, too, Mom." I smiled at her.

Daddy was just now waking up when we got there. He had to leave pretty soon. "Wow, Sarah. You look as pretty as the day I met you."

"You look as handsome, too." She smiled at him.

We had brought dinner home and he joined us at the table. We bowed our heads and prayed over the meal and I served the food. We had gotten a family pack at Miller's. It was a seafood place. My dad absolutely loved fish and my mom wanted to surprise him.

After he left for work, I cleaned up the dining room while my mom slept. It had been a good day.

Mom had said she wanted to visit her granddaughters soon but since they were sick with the chicken pox, I knew it would be another two weeks before we could. That is one thing about cancer. You have to be careful with immune systems and everything because it can make the patient sicker. But I had text my brother to tell the twins not to worry. Aunt Lyric would see them soon and Grandmama was okay.

I figured while my mom slept, I would go mail Huntley the letter I wrote him and send him one of the pictures I took at the mall. I happily smiled at the camera and you could not tell I had all this stress and worry on me but somehow I knew he knew. The smile was not fake as I had a blast with my mom and I had wanted to look pretty for Huntley but you can tell in my eyes the stress I had been feeling ever since the doctor had said those words to my mom. "You have cancer."

Cancer, what an awful word? My niece Stacey says she is going to be a scientist when she grows up and find a cure. I hope she does. Wouldn't that be perfect? I know the first person who would get the antidote would be my mom.

Huntley

Dear Lyric,

I have exciting news to tell you. First though, I will answer your questions. Thank you for the picture. Don't worry; I can send your nieces an autographed photo, too. Aw, from your letter, I thought you never heard of me till you read my book on my dad.

I love my book series Sleuthing Sam but I want to branch out more and do other stuff and your letter was just reassurance that I can reach more people with my words.

But wow, your picture is really pretty. Plain ole you? I don't think so. You are really something.

Hayley Mills, huh? My favorite movie she is in is That Darn Cat......but my favorite movie altogether is Galaxy Quest. It is so funny. Have you seen it?

I know it is tough dealing with a sick parent but reading the Bible and praying helps. Surround yourself with friends. I hope my letters help some and hope your mom is doing okay.

Your poem was really something and heartfelt. You captured the breaking heart news perfectly. They say stuff gets easier with time but I think whoever said that never faced this.

But now onto my exciting news! They are going to be making Sleuthing Sam into a movie! I go on tour next month and then, when I get back I get to discuss and collaborate with the screenplay writer. I am told it is already done but I just have to approve of it.

Hopefully, it works out great. Maybe I can get your nieces tickets to the premiere. I looked at my tour's schedule and saw that one of my stops is in Nashville. How far is that away from you? It looks like I will be there the third week. I would love to meet your nieces and give them an autograph copy of my book in person. But no pressure on you since we just met,

Hope to hear from you, soon!

Your friend,

Huntley Crisp

Huntley

When I told my mom about Sleuthing Sam becoming a movie, she was absolutely thrilled. "Wow, Huntley," she exclaimed. "My son, the famous writer. Your dad would be so proud of you."

I smiled back at her, hoping she was right. "Will you be okay watching Sam when I am on tour?" I asked. She nodded. She leaned over and petted Sam's head gently. "Sam and I are going to have a good ole time, aren't we?"

I couldn't believe it, I was going to be on tour next week. The days had flown. I checked my schedule when we would be in Tennessee and had written Lyric the details.

I told her no pressure on her but I would be willing to meet her nieces and I had silently thought to myself, meet her. We exchanged numbers and my heart about jumped when I saw Lyric's text. All it said was Just wanted to say hi. But I was absolutely thrilled.

"Who is that?" My mom glanced at me as she smiled knowingly.

I had mentioned Lyric and I were writing. Even though I insisted we were just friends, she just said, "Sure, you are."

My mom was always wanting to set me up with "the perfect girl." She had seen Lyric's picture as I had put it in a picture frame on my desk. "Lyric's awfully pretty."

I knew romance was the last thing on our minds as she was overwhelmed with taking care of her mom and I was about to be slammed and busy with the upcoming tour. But I had to admit her picture was captivating.

I had started doodling Lyric and decided to send her the picture. I titled the picture Lyric's Lilacs as I had drew her picking flowers.

Lyric's Lilacs By Huntley Crisp

It just came to me to write a short story about a girl taking care of her mom that was sick and picked flowers to cheer her mom up. Maybe I could make it into a book and dedicate it to Lyric. I knew I would be swamped with my tour so right now, I knew it was going to be on the back burner for now.

I didn't want to quit writing letters to Lyric but we figured with my tour, it would be best to exchange emails and numbers. I know emails are basically like letters but for some reason reading her handwritten words made my heart soar. Her email was so pretty being, lyricsrainysong@gmail.com. Mine was a little more simple as it was just Sleuthingsam@gmail.com for my book series and dog.

They sent me the promotional poster for the movie and I had to admit I was impressed. They had kept the appearance of my character the same and I couldn't wait to see the movie. They had decided to release it in December but no date was on it just in case production was delayed.

Wow, my book was going to become a movie! I was so excited! I took a picture of the poster and sent it to Lyric on my cell.

She replied, Wow, that is so cool looking. My nieces are going to flip!

I included with her next letter an autograph copy picture of myself to her nieces. I gave them one each because I figured that way they would not fight over it. On Stacey's I wrote, Sleuthing Sam found out you wanted to be a scientist and when you do, he might ask you for help on his cases. Lyric had mentioned it in one of her letters and so I kind of wanted to personalize this to my fans and I realized I didn't know much about Stella.

I knew it was random but I texted Lyric, What did Stella want to do when she grew up?

Lyric was puzzled why I had asked but told me she wants to be a detective.

"Perfect," I thought as I addressed Stella's picture, Maybe Sleuthing Sam and you can team up one day to solve mysteries.

I texted Lyric she would find out when she got her next letter from me. I knew with my tour, it probably would be the last letter I wrote for awhile. But at least there was always email. I loved getting letters from her but I am sure I would love emails, too.

Lyric

Subject: Hi
To: Sleuthingsam@gmail.com
From: lyricsrainysong@gmail.com

Hi, Huntley,

This is weird emailing you since we communicate so well in our letters. But my nieces were thrilled with the pictures you sent them. They were like how did Sleuthing Sam find out? So now, they are convinced he is real and really solving mysteries all about them. I didn't have the heart to tell them it was because of me.

Mom is getting tired a lot lately. We try to do stuff but the treatment is wearing her down. It is funny how you said that you start your tour soon. Mom quits her radiation treatment and then, they are going to doing radiation implants. I am dreading that so much. So is my mom. They even told us, we cannot visit her for a whole week, because the radiation is not reduced so we could be affected. I don't like that, but at least we can talk to her. Did your dad have anything like that?

I know you are busy but I am probably going to bombard you with emails when that happens to keep my mind off things? Hope I won't drive you insane.

I haven't seen *Galaxy Quest* but maybe I can give it a try.

We are planning a trip to the aquarium Saturday. They have a new butterfly exhibit I can't wait to check out. I love butterflies. Maybe one day you can check it out, too. My mom is excited we get to do something with the twins. She had really been missing them because of them having the chicken pox.
Have fun on tour!

Your friend,
Lyric

I was so happy that we were going to the aquarium. The Butterfly Garden was my favorite thing there. We hadn't been there in forever and they had added to the exhibit and so I couldn't wait to see what it looked like.

If you stand really still and hold out your hand, a butterfly will land on you. It is the coolest thing ever. My grandmother always said if that happens you get a wish. So if that so happens I am going to wish my mom not to be sick anymore. Of course, prayers work, too.

Our family was all there. My dad, my mom, the twins, my brother, and his wife. We took a wheelchair in case my mom got too tired and the twins were fighting over who was going to "push Grandmama." They ended up taking turns. We checked the butterflies first.

I held out my hand as just as a butterfly landed in my outstretch hands, it was startled by Stella trying to grab it. "Stella, that scares the butterflies. Try to stay still."

She did as told and a yellow one with beautiful markings landed on her. "What do I do? What do I do?" She hissed.

"Make a wish." I smiled at her. She closed her eyes and it flapped away.

"So how do I know it will come true?" Stella asked, with wide eyes.

"Butterfly wishes always come true." I told her and she squealed. I am not really sure what she wished for. But she was surely excited.

We got to see all sorts of sea creatures from sharks to sting rays to big box turtles. It was feeding time for the sharks and my nieces cheered when they saw the sharks devour fish showing a little blood. Ew, that was the last thing I wanted to see.

My mom was having a great time. I was so happy that we got to enjoy this with her.

I thought I would get a small something for Huntley for being so nice to the twins. I settled on a stuffed little turtle. It was so cute. The twins each begged for a stuffed animal too and their parents gave in, buying two sharks. One pink and one blue. At least these couldn't bite you and show any blood.

"So, Stella, what did you wish for?" My mom asked her as she pushed her wheelchair.

"The only thing that I really really really want."

"What's that?"

"For you to be better, Grandmama. That is all I need." With that, Stella wrapped her tiny arms around my mom.

Good. Stella had not wasted her wish. And the best part Butterfly Wishes Always Came True.

Huntley

Subject: Hi Back!
To:lyricsrainysong@gmail.com
From: Sleuthingsam@gmail.com

Hi, Lyric, I am so happy that emails didn't dampen the connection of what we had. If anything it made it stronger. Butterflies, huh? You remind me of a butterfly. Pretty but strong and determined.

As you know, the first stop on my tour was in Miami. You should see one dude here who was in line with his kids. He was so weird. He had on a trench coat and a hat pulled over his eyes. He looked like a secret agent. He went up to me and I kid you not, he said something weird like I am undercover, here to get your autograph. Is Sleuthing Sam with you? He was so weird. But you meet all kinds of people on tour.

I understand if you need to blow up my phone or write me like crazy. I know how it is dealing with the cancer stuff. No, my dad, did not have to have implants. That is scary sounding but it sounds like in the long run it will help your mom.

How about a quiz till the next time I write? It will be fun.

1. What is your full name? Huntley Todd Crisp (Feel special because I don't reveal my middle name to a lot of people)

2. When is your birthday? April 12th

3. What is your favorite food? Spaghetti

4. What is your favorite book? (I won't be offended if you don't say mine...lol) *The Wind in the Willows*

5. Do you have any pets? Just Sleuthing Sam. I am glad I adopted him.

Not much of a quiz, huh? But we know so much about one another already, so I was stumped a little on the questions. I will be praying for your mom and you. I know it will be tough in the moments ahead but you got this. Trust me but more importantly, trust God. He has got a comforting hand on you and your mom.

Wish me happy touring!

Your friend,

Huntley

P.S. I will write when I can but it might be in between stops on my tour. Text me all you want.

My agent was rushing around like a chicken with its head cut off. "Calm down, Leah. It is just a Meet and Greet." I told her.

"The place hasn't confirmed us though. They were supposed to send me the details already." Leah said. We had moved from Miami to our next stop in Atlanta. I knew we going to be going from town to town to town but I was dying to rest soon.

I was supposed to do a Meet and Greet at a local book store there. They had already started advertising my movie. I called it my movie because well, it was based on my books, wasn't it? I peeked at the schedule to see when we would be in Tennessee. I knew Lyric was dealing with a lot but I just had to see her, so one way or the other I was going to work it into my schedule.

We headed to Tennessee the day after tomorrow. Cool. I figured I would surprise Lyric with that news. I knew her mom was about to start the radiation treatment implants soon so Lyric was probably a worried mess. During the tours, I always had a little free time to do some exploring and window shopping. And I do mean little. Leah was strict with my time but it turns out the stop in Atlanta, the meet and greet fell through due to the store owner had became sick and failed to tell us. So that means we could either stay in Atlanta or head to Tennessee. I told Leah that I had a friend to stop in and see and could we please go ahead and head to Tennessee. She eventually agreed.

We actually decided to go by train to Tennessee. I had my own private room, called a sleeper cabin. Leah had booked the seats and we were on our way to Tennessee. We had a driver that took us around to the cities in the tour but since Atlanta got rescheduled, we had to make other arrangements. He had family in Atlanta so he had stayed there for the weekend and was going to meet us that Friday.

Four hours later, we had arrived in Nashville. I looked up how far Chattanooga was and it said two and a half hours. Since our scheduling for the tour didn't begin till Friday, I decided I would go ahead and see Lyric. I promised Leah I would be back before the Book Signing begin. Surprisingly, she agreed. I figured I would rent a car and head there. For some reason, I felt I had to see Lyric. My Porsche SUV was at home with my mom and dog but thankfully, it was quite easy to rent a car. Leah went with me to rent the car and I drove to the hotel. We decided to check in and then, I was going to head out to see Lyric.

It was really nice. Not to brag but I have made a lot of money on my books so we were able to stay at a 4 star hotel. Our rooms were huge.

I decided to put away my luggage and call my mom to check on Sam. She assured me everything was going okay and wanted to know how the tour was going. I told her everything and she asked me where I was. When I said Tennessee, she started in on me about Lyric. "So does this mean what I think? You actually going to meet this girl?" She teased me.

"Maybe," I replied back. I didn't want to tell her yet I wanted to drive down to surprise Lyric. I didn't want to jinx our first meeting. We hung up and I decided to get ready to meet this girl. I never felt so close to anyone but we never met. I figured I would surprise her and not tell her I was coming. I knew she was having a hard week, not being able to visit her mom.

I showered and then changed into khakis and a nice blue dress shirt. I wanted to look presentable when I met her for the first time. Wow, for the first time. I was going to meet this amazing girl. I was excited and nervous at the same time.

I figured I might want to stay in Cambridge a couple of days so I gathered a few clothes in a bag I had. But at least if I didn't stay there, I could just come back to the hotel and relax. I know some people would think I am just blowing money but I just had to see her. I knew she was dealing with a lot and had to be there for her. It was just like a feeling I had.

Here goes nothing as I drove towards the open road.

Lyric

Subject: Quiz Answers
To: Sleuthingsam@gmail.com
From: lyricsrainysong@gmail.com

1. What is your full name? Your middle name is cool. But my full name is Lyric Rain Sumner. No making fun.

2. When is your birthday? November 5th

3. What is your favorite food? Soup, to be more specific Potato Soup lol I know that is weird saying it is my fav food but it has always been.

4. What is your favorite book? Your book meant a lot to me but *Jane Eyre.*

5. Do you have any pets? No, there is a fish I named in the Chemotherapy lobby called Skipper. He is bright orange and keeps me company when I wait for my mom.

I feel so sad. My mom started her radiation implants Monday and she gets to go home Thursday. It is scary that they are saying she is radioactive. But I am glad that the treatment will soon be over and I am hoping that this means she will get 100 percent better.

I guess you are on tour, visiting your fans. I hope you are doing okay. I miss you. I wish we could talk while my mom is in the hospital but I know you are swamped.

Hope to hear from you soon!

Your friend,

Lyric

My dad was busy with work and my brother and his wife invited me over so I wouldn't be too bored at home by myself. We face timed with my mom on Skype. Thankfully, they let her have her laptop. She had her cellphone, laptop, and Bible. She told us not to worry as God would take care of her.

We were glad we got to see my mom. Stacey and Stella performed a little dance for my mom. She clapped at the end as they squealed tah-dah. She then said she had to rest. So she bid us good night and hung up the phone.

Suzy fixed grilled chicken with mixed veggies. I had to admit it was pretty good even though I didn't have much of an appetite. After dinner, we decided to watch a movie. We decided on *The Incredibles*. The twins wanted to see it.

After the movie, I decided to head home because I had to admit I was pretty exhausted. Maybe I would email Huntley and then go to bed. I couldn't wait till this week was over and my mom was back at home.

It was Tuesday so only two more days. I couldn't wait. I went home, took a shower and got ready for bed. I heard the doorbell ring and wondered who on Earth could it be. I grabbed my robe, tied it around me and headed to the door. "Who is it?" I called out, looking through the peep hole.

I was stunned. There in the flesh it was Huntley. I opened the door, wishing I knew he was coming as I was not ready for company at all.

I opened the door. "Huntley? I thought you were in Atlanta."

"It got canceled so I was able to head to Tennessee early and decided to stop in and say hi to you. I didn't mean to get her so late but it took longer getting here than I thought."

We hugged and I realized my hair was a little damp from the shower and got his shirt a little wet. "I am so sorry." I said.

"It's okay. I wanted to surprise you because I know you are having a hard week, not being able to visit your mom."

I smiled at him. "This is definitely the best surprise." I invited him inside. "If you excuse me, I am going to go change. I was tired but now, I am wide awake."

"Sure, I know I was the last person you expected." Huntley said.

I went into my room and changed into capris and a t-shirt that said Paris. It was not fancy or anything and rather casual but I figured he already seen me in my bathrobe so I had to look better than that.

"I am glad you are not upset I came to see you." Huntley said.

"Just surprised; that's all." I smiled. "This is an awesome surprise. Oh, that reminds me, I will be right back." I hadn't mailed his sea turtle yet because I knew he was on tour but now I could give it to him in person. I had left it on my bed. I went to get it and then, gave it to him.

"I got this from the aquarium for you. It's not much but it was cute."

"I love it. Thank you. My tour isn't till Friday so if you are available, I'd love to hang out. I figure you could use the cheering up while your mom is in the hospital. She comes home Thursday, right? I will stay around and meet her, too, and then, I have to get going back or Leah will strangle me. Oh and I brought new Sleuthing Sam toys for the twins. They just came out. ”

I was floored he drove all this way to meet me. “I'd love to hang out with you.” I wanted to invite him to sleep over on our couch but I knew I couldn't since I didn't ask permission from my parents. And my dad would be upset if a strange guy was sleeping on our couch.

As reading my mind, he said, “Don't worry. I can get a hotel. You had no idea I was coming.”

I felt embarrassed but knew that was the best decision because I hadn't asked my dad and my brother and his wife would feel wary of this stranger in their house being near the twins.

True, he was a stranger in a way but I never felt closer to anyone. I really was wide awake now as I loved to hear the sound of his voice and look into his blue eyes.

"I think I am a little hungry from all that traveling. Do you think we can go get a bite to eat?" Huntley asked me.

"Sure," I said. "We can go in my car since you are tired of driving." I teased. "Besides, I know the way."

"I don't know; my mom taught me to never to get in a car with strangers. Especially good looking ones."

I blushed at that but we piled into my small Dodge Dart anyways. He looked relieved to finally not be driving. We went to a 24/7 diner where we talked and talked. It was just the same as our letters and emails. It felt so surreal. It was eleven o'clock so not too late but I didn't want the time to end.

Once, a man who was rather on the chubby side sat at a table next to us and when he got up, he knocked coffee all over our table. "I am so sorry. Let me get you another...."

He stopped mid-sentence. "Oh, my gosh, do you know who you are? You are that writer with that dog, right? Huntley Crisp?"

"I am." Huntley smiled at him.

"Will you pose for a picture with me? I can't wait to tell my kids. They have all your dog books."

Huntley just said sure and I ended up taking the picture on the guy's antique cell phone. Huntley turned to the guy and asked him if he would take a picture of us on his cellphone. Huntley put his arm around me and we smiled as we posed for the picture.

I felt like my head was spinning. It felt so good to be in Huntley's arms. But as soon as the picture was taken, Huntley went back to normal position. We had ordered pancakes and coffee.

I drove back home after we were done eating. Huntley paid for both of us. I didn't even ask him to, he just grabbed the check. He told me it was to thank me for the turtle I had given him.

I saw the clock read 12:12. My grandmother always said if the numbers matched you get a wish. My grandmother was big on wishing. I was about to wish for my mom to be alright again, when I heard Huntley point that out.

"It's 12:12, so we each get a wish. Do you know what I wish for?" I shook my head no and was surprised when Huntley brushed my lips with his in the most tender most heart felt kiss I ever received. "It already came true." He said, when we finally broke apart.

It was the most perfect kiss. And I was in love. Now what would make it even more perfect, if my mom would get better. That is the one wish I really hoped would come true.

Huntley

Subject: Hi
To:lyricsrainysong@gmail.com
From: Sleuthingsam@gmail.com

Hi, Lyric. I am so glad we met. It seems almost like a dream, doesn't it? I went ahead and got a hotel room here even though I had checked in Nashville. I just did not feel like driving. I was pretty tired after I left you. I am just glad I packed a few things with me so I wouldn't be going back and forth.

So your mom comes home tomorrow, right? I am so glad for you.

I figured you could show me around town today and then, I will meet your mom and head back. I wish I could spend more time but Leah will strangle me if I don't make it back for the tour. And besides, I promised her. I always keep my word.

I am glad that our meeting was just like our emails and letters. I was worried that things would change but I am relieved that didn't happen. If anything I feel our connection is even stronger.

I would love to meet your family and I have your nieces' gifts I would love to give them. Just text me when and where you want to meet.

Your friend,

Huntley

I left Lyric's about one in the morning. We shared the most amazing kiss. I was head over heels for this girl and the kiss just deepened our connection. I could tell she wanted to invite me in but we just stayed out in the car talking, looking at the stars. She lives out in the country and so the night sky was very visible. But the two stars I was staring at were in her eyes.

I kissed her goodnight and I headed toward my rental car. I debated for a second going back to my hotel room in Nashville but I was too tired so I went ahead and got a hotel here in Cambridge. It was a cheaper hotel than what I had in Nashville and I knew I was wasting money but Lyric was worth it.

I immediately crawled into bed and fell asleep with my clothes on. I was too tired to change. I dreamed about my dad and seeing him in heaven. I realized that him getting sick, and dying, and me writing the book is the main reason I had Lyric in my life.

It was like my dad and God gave me this incredible gift. I realized that is what this driving force of having to see Lyric was all about. I knew Lyric was hurting because of her mom. I had been there before and I didn't want her to feel the pain I had.

I know God does everything in His own timing. And when I lost my dad, I felt like my heart had been ripped apart but meeting Lyric, it begun to heal.

When I woke up, I saw that I had a text message on my phone. "Hi, Huntley."

I felt like a giddy teenager as I texted back the girl of my dreams. "Hi, Lyric. So when are we meeting?"

"Well, how about you meet me at my house at noon and then, we will head to my brother's house and you can be introduced to the famous future scientist and detective."

"Sounds like a plan." I was about to type more but then my cell started to ring. It was Lyric. It was so weird but we never actually talked on the phone. "Hello?"

"Hi, Huntley. I just had to hear your sexy voice again." Lyric said. I could almost picture her saying that as I closed my eyes.

"Well, you will hear it in a few hours. You mean you couldn't wait?" I joked.

"I just had to tell you how glad I am we met and it meant a lot you coming all the way to see me."

"What are friends for?" I told her.

"Um, well, with that kiss I say it is safe to say we are little more than that. Right?" She joked. I could tell she was nervous asking me that but she still wanted to know my response.

"True, I would definitely say we are more. I am glad that I met you, Lyric."

"Me, too, Huntley." She said, softly. We talked a few more minutes and then she said she had to go call her mom. Speaking of, I better call my mom, too, and tell her what was happening.

The first thing out of her mouth was, "So did you meet Lyric?"

"That is a fine howdy do to say to your son. How about did you get there safe? Are you okay?"

"Well, clearly, you got there safe. I am talking to you. But Sam and I are wanting to know the details."

"How is Sam? How are you?" I asked, still ignoring the questions.

"We are fine. So did you meet the girl or not?"

"Lyric and I met, Mom. We hit it off. I am seeing her later, today."

I was greeted by a squeal in my ear. "I knew it. I knew it!"

Mom and I talked a few minutes more and then, I thought I better get ready and meet Lyric. I showered got dressed and headed to her place.

She was a knockout as she had dressed up a little and I took pleasure knowing the fact that she wanted to look nice for me. Her long dark hair hung loose down her back and she wore a spaghetti-strapped blue and white striped dress and sandals. Her toes were perfectly polished and her natural beauty shone with the light makeup she wore.

In her hair, she wore a blue and white striped hairband that matched her dress that had a blue bow on it.

She smiled at me as she gave me a hug. "See, now, that I knew you were coming over, I had time to look presentable."

"I thought you liked my surprise." I teased her.

"Oh, I did. But I usually don't want to open the door in my bathrobe." She laughed.

"Sorry about that," I said.

"I forgive you." She kissed me on the cheek and we decided to get going. She explained her dad was asleep since he had to work late again that night. She would introduce me to him later.

She told me to follow her and we would go to her brother's house. She had already told him and his wife we were coming. Suzy was able to stay at home and watch her girls while Lyric's brother worked as a security guard at a bank. He worked later that night so he was able to meet me.

So I followed her in my rental car to her brother's house. It was a nice blue house with a bay window. Lyric knocked on the door and a lady answered with curly blonde hair I presumed was Suzy. She invited us in the house. "It is so nice to meet you, Mr. Crisp. Thank you for taking the time to meet the girls. They love your books."

"Call me Huntley, please." I told her. Kyle entered the room, then. "It is a pleasure meeting you. The twins are waking up from their nap soon and will be so excited to meet you."

I had the stuffed Sleuthing Sam dogs with me. I hadn't mentioned the movie to many people but I was going to finally tell the girls today. Lyric promised she would let me tell them. I didn't want to make them think Sleuthing Sam was not real because in a way he was. Sam helped me with those books just as much.

We sat in the living room while we talked. I was kind of nervous meeting Lyric's family but they put me right at ease. I noticed Suzy had taken Lyric to the side and was talking to her. I wondered if they were talking about me. I overheard one sentence and knew that was exactly the direction their conversation was going. The phrase you dressed up for him, didn't you made me smile.

I turned back to Kyle who was asking me if it was hard to get started writing books and what else had I written besides Sleuthing Sam. Apparently, he did not read the book I had written about my dad. But, I told him I wanted to branch out, do other stories.

He seemed surprised when I mentioned, *How To Deal With A Loved One Having Cancer.* "I didn't know that is how the two of you met. Lyric, why didn't you tell me that? I thought you started writing this guy for the twins?"

"Writing who for us?" Stella yawned. She was her mom made over with little blonde curls down her back. She gaped when she came into the living room and stared right at me. "Stacey! Come quick! Sleuthing Sam's owner is in our living room!"

"You are joking, right?" Stacey came into view. The sisters were identical with the same wide-eyed expressions staring at me.

"Hi, your aunt told me you guys were big fans so I wanted to give you these Sleuthing Sam stuffed dogs." I told them.

"So is Sam made up?" Stella asked, almost tearfully.

"Nope, he is as real as can be. He is actually at my house. My mom is house sitting my place and him for me." The girls seemed to find this fascinating. They wanted me to sign their whole collection. They grabbed my hand and led me to their room and on their bookshelf, sure enough, all 44 books of Sam were on the shelf.

"You weren't kidding when you said they were fans, huh." I told Lyric who had followed us.

"Aunt Lyric, why didn't you tell us you knew Sam's author?" Stacey pounded her aunt with questions.

Lyric tried to look innocent from her accuser as she pointed at me and said, "He wanted to tell you."

I personalized a couple of the books for the girls and then, I just signed my name. Believe me, I love my fans, but giving autographs is tiring after awhile. We went back into the living room.

"I have exciting news to tell you all. Sleuthing Sam's first movie comes out in December and I will get you all tickets. Will you like that?"

The twins were jumping up for joy and I could tell their parents were thrilled I had made their girls' day. "What a birthday present!"

At that I looked puzzled but Suzy explained their birthday was that month.

"Their birthday is in December so they start school next year.   In Tennessee, you have to be five before the school year starts or you can't start school, which I hate them getting a late start like that so I have been teaching them. They already know how to read and count to one hundred. They are so smart." Suzy told me, beaming about her girls. "We always take turn reading Sleuthing Sam books! No joke, they read them to me."

"Well, it was definitely an honor and a privilege to meet such sweet and smart girls." I said and the girls beamed.

Lyric spoke up, "Isn't it time to call Grandmama?" She asked the girls and they cheered. They gathered in the kitchen and Kyle got on his laptop and they called Mrs. Sumner through Skype, turning the webcam on. They introduced Lyric's mom to me. She had a few gray strands among her dark hair and looked tired but you could tell that is where Lyric got her beauty from.

She smiled at me and said she heard so much about me. We didn't get to talk much as all her family wanted to talk to her. They talked a few minutes more and Lyric said she better be getting home to bring her dad food. We had already planned we were going to eat at Nell's, which was Lyric's favorite restaurant that she really wanted to show me and get a plate to go for her dad and introduce me.

It felt so weird meeting her family when we just met ourselves yesterday but I was enjoying every bit of it. Her family was great and Lyric was definitely great.

I definitely would be sad to leave Thursday night but I knew the tour would need to get back on track. We bid goodbye and headed to Nell's. Lyric in her car, me in my rental one.

Thank you for being so sweet to my family!

You're welcome.
They are wonderful.

You're pretty wonderful.

You trying to make me blush?

Yeah, payback for making me answer the door in my robe.

You said you forgave me for that.
Remember?

So I did. I don't know.
It sounded good.

When do you pick up your mom?

Early. Eight o'clock.
I can't wait to see her.

I bet. But I better let you go so you
can get some rest. But text me
tomorrow, okay?

Okay. I am getting pretty sleepy.
But I hate to let you go.

No worries.
We can meet in Dreamland.

Sounds like a plan.
Have sweet dreams.

Well, since I will be dreaming about you.
Of course.

Now, who is trying
to make who blush?

You caught me, lol.
We better get some rest.
Nighters, Lyric.

Night, Huntley.
Sweet Dreams.

I sighed happily looking at my text messages. I scrolled through all of my and Huntley's texts and I absolutely melted into happiness as my heart did a little flutter. I was deep in like with this guy, maybe almost on the verge of love. And to think we bonded over cancer.

But I was very happy with how the day went and best part of all was my mom was going to get to come home tomorrow morning. Huntley promised to meet us and then, he had to head back. Oh, he said he had a surprise for both me and my mom. I had no idea what it could be.

So today had been perfect. After meeting my brother and his family, we headed to Nell's. It is my favorite restaurant and I wanted him to experience it. They have the best potato soup so maybe that is why I like soup so much. But it is definitely yummy.

I felt like I was in a movie where guy meets girl and she is in a whirlwind romance. I have never fell so quickly for a guy before and I knew I was using this guy as an emotional crutch with my mom being sick. No, that was not exactly true. We were using each other. We were thrown into this world where parents got sick and we had experienced the trials and hardships of what that meant. He on one hand had lost his dad. I at least had my mom but it felt a lot easier knowing someone had faced this.

Sure, I had my other caregiver friends but I felt disconnected, almost like a bystander looking in when I heard their story. With Huntley's book, I experienced his journey and it made mine a little easier. And of course, reading my Bible and leaning on God helped, too. I really think God sent me Huntley to help me during the absence of my mom. I don't know if I could have gotten through without him. And I know I couldn't have gotten through without God. My mom always told me, Never let go of Jesus and I did not intend to.

After Nell's, we went to my house to meet my dad. I had brought him a to go plate and he really appreciated it. He told Huntley that it was a pleasure meeting him and he had planned to read his book, too. I could tell they liked one another as they got into old Navy stories. Apparently, Huntley's uncle had been in the Navy also and so they talked for what seemed like hours on that subject.

After my dad went to work, Huntley and I were alone. We decided to watch *Galaxy Quest.* He had packed it in hopes of showing it to me. He was definitely right. It was hilarious. I made us some microwave popcorn and our hands brushed together when we both reached for a kernel.

"If you wanted to hold hands, all you had to do was ask." Huntley teased me.

After the movie, I asked Huntley if he cared if I called my mom. He told me that was fine as I dialed her cell. She told me she loved me and I was glad that it was not on speaker phone when she gave me the lecture about not letting anyone "hurt me" meaning, don't let guys touch me.

I think that would be pretty rotten if I did that anyways with my mom in the hospital and besides I didn't plan on sex before marriage anyway. My parents had taught me better than that but I knew it did not look right being in a house alone with a guy even if we weren't doing anything, so I asked him if he wanted to take a walk with me after I got off the phone.

It was so wonderful, walking hand in hand with him. It was a cool spring night and so it was a little chilly.

"Lyric," Huntley started to say.

"What, Huntley?"

"I am glad we met; that's all. I think God knew I needed you. No, that we needed each other."

"Yes, it is something out of the movies. What we have is so magical."

"You are magical. I am glad I made the trip out here." Huntley told me as he pulled me, deep in a kiss. "And don't worry; I am not the kind of guy who will hurt you."

"Oh, my gosh, you heard what my mom said?" I gasped.

"Well, she did say it kind of loud. But no worries. She is just worried about you. I think it's cute." He laughed and I realized that was what I liked best about him. Sure, he was cute with dreamy eyes and a sexy smile but his sense of humor made him so attractive. And I knew I needed laughter in my life instead of constant worry all the time.

We bid goodnight and then, when he got back to his hotel, we texted one another. And I definitely had sweet dreams after talking to him.

The next morning, I got up at six, showered and dressed and got ready for the day. This was going to be a great day as Mama would get to come home! No more radiation and no more chemo!

I went to her room, and she was sitting up in bed. I had left a change of clothes for her to change into and so she was fully dressed and a nurse had fixed her hair. Sighs of relief came over me as I haven't seen my mom look this healthy in a long time.

I prayed a thank you prayer and they let me pull the car around as one of the nurses pushed her in a wheelchair. We sat her in the front seat and we were on our way home. Next month was her checkup and I knew the cancer had to be gone. For God answers prayers!

Huntley and Lyric's texts

When do you want to meet me
at your house?

How about noon?

Sounds like a plan.
How is your mom?

She is doing okay.
Just a little tired.

Well, hopefully she will get some
rest and be a whole lot better.

I hope you're right.

Just trust on God.
Everything will work out.

I need to lean on God more
instead of
being such a worrywart.

I can be a worrywart, too. But we
both need to Trust God.

I better get going
but see you at noon.

Okay, Lyric. See you then.

I knew I had to head back tonight but I was rather sad I was saying goodbye to Lyric but her mom was coming home today so I knew she would be okay. But I was definitely going to miss her. I never been in a long distance relationship before and I knew it was going to be tough but Lyric was worth it.

I couldn't wait to show Lyric my surprise and her mom. I never gave her the drawing I had doodled of her and so in the little spare time I had, I had started the story and finished it and was going to publish it after I talked to Leah and have her send it to my publisher. *Lyric's Lilacs* was dedicated to Lyric and her mom. I had printed off a copy to show them.

So I headed to Lyric's around noon and knocked on the door. She told me not to ring the doorbell as not to wake her dad. He had taken the day off to spend with his wife but he had a long night at work so was still fast asleep. She answered looking pretty as ever. She invited me in. Her mom was in the living room sitting on the couch.

"Hi, Mrs. Sumner. How are you feeling?" I asked her.

"Much, much better. I heard so much about you. It is so nice to meet you. Treat my daughter right, okay?"

"Mom!" Lyric hissed, clearly embarrassed.

"I will, ma'am. You can count on me. She is a remarkable girl."

"You guys are going to make me die of embarrassment; quit!" Lyric sighed, collapsing in an armchair with her face in her hands.

"Before you do that, let me give you my surprise," I told her, giving her a copy of my story.

"What is this?" She asked, flipping through the pages.

"I wrote you and your mom a story. It is a short story about a girl taking care of her mom."

"Oh, my gosh, look, Mom." She went over to the couch and showed her mom the story.

"That is very sweet of you, Huntley," Mrs. Sumner said.

"After my tour, I will get it published and give you a real copy of it. Look at the dedication."

Lyric flipped to the dedication where it said, To my friend, Lyric and her mom. I will always cherish our times together.

"Aw, look, Mom, it is dedicated to both of us." Lyric pointed to the dedication. "I am sure my mom and I will enjoy reading it. It means a lot you dedicating the book to us.”

“You’re welcome. I wanted to show you how much your letters and everything meant.” I told her. I wanted to kiss her and hold her in my arms but didn’t since her mom was right there.

“When do you head back?”

“I actually got to head back now. Leah has been wanting me to get back. She arranged something tonight before the Meet and Greet tomorrow. I just wanted to tell you goodbye before I left.” I told Lyric. I didn’t want to tell her bye but I knew I had responsibilities that I had to attend to.

“Oh,” Lyric said, disappointingly. “Well, let me walk you to your car.” She said, softly. Her voice kind of broke when she said that as I could tell she was not wanting me to go.

"Sure. It was nice meeting you, Mrs. Sumner. I am glad you are doing alright."

"With time, I will be doing much better. God will take care of me. But keep me in your prayers."

"I will, ma'am."

"Have a safe trip, Huntley." She called out when Lyric and I walked out together.

"Thank you. Pray that I do." I called back.

Lyric walked to the car door as I got in the driver's seat. "Huntley, I couldn't have gotten through this week without you."

"Sure you could. Don't forget you are stronger than you think," I declared. "And you have God. But I am glad that I could help some."

"Don't fool yourself; you helped a lot." Lyric said. She leaned in the car and kissed me. "Stay safe, okay? Write me when you can."

"You know I will." I told her bye and kissed her one more time and soon I was on the road again heading to Nashville. I was going to miss her. Our meeting seemed almost dreamlike. But it had been perfect.

Now to get on back with the tour and then, I would get to see Sam and my mom again. I couldn't wait.

Lyric

Subject: I miss you!
To: Sleuthingsam@gmail.com
From: lyricsrainysong@gmail.com

Hi, Huntley. You just left a little while ago. Oh my gosh, I read the story you wrote. I am touched you wrote it for me. My mom loved it, too.

I have a little time for myself because Daddy took my mom out to eat. He said he wanted to treat her since she had been cooped up in the hospital. Wow, I didn't think I would miss you as much as I do. You made this week so much better for me.

I am glad we are going to stay in touch with one another and our connection is just as strong as ever. I feel like I am falling in love with you. I hope that isn't too soon to say.

Love, Lyric

122

I had to tell Huntley how I was feeling. I was nervous about telling him since I never spoke how I was feeling aloud but surely, he felt the same way. The story was sweet that he had written. It was a girl who was taking care of her mom who was sick and every morning she would pick flowers lilacs for her.

And one day, she had found a magical flower that grew off by itself. It was still a lilac but when she picked that and gave it to her mom, she was instantly healed. Then, the next day when they went to church, the pastor revealed he had planted the flower and it was through the power of prayer the lady was healed.

I was able to read it since I had time to myself. I felt even closer to this man. I loved the fact, he loved God. It made me love him all the more and I felt God knew

I needed this guy and he answered my prayer I did not even know I had. True, he answered my prayer about my mom, but sending Huntley into my life was just what I needed, too.

I heard my phone ding and picked it up to see a text message. My heart skipped a beat when I saw it was Huntley.

"I don't have much time because the fan meet is about to start but I read your email and I love you, too." The text read, making my day.

"You do?" I texted back.

"Of course, silly. But I really do have to go now. Talk to you soon." I stared at Huntley's text and smiled.

God knew what I needed. My mom was going to be alright and I had Huntley in my life. I decided I would spend some time in prayer and thank God for His blessings. He definitely deserved to be thanked with all He had done for me...and my mom.

Over the next few weeks, Huntley had been swamped with the tour so he did not write much but I knew he was thinking of me with a small email here and there and texts.

I missed him but I had begin giving piano lessons to students. I decided not to go back to work at the office in case my mom needed me. But I loved giving piano lessons to young students. It was my passion, playing the piano and I even thought about writing a song.

My mom was absolutely thrilled with the story Huntley had written. She had me read it to her again and again. I didn't mind. We were both happy the power of prayer definitely worked wonders and Huntley had captured that perfectly in his story.

I couldn't wait till he had more time. I missed him bunches. But all I could do was wait. Man, I hate waiting. But maybe I could start writing the song that was going through my head. I really enjoyed playing the piano and so I thought I would give it a try.

Huntley

Dear Lyric,

So now I am back at home and working on the movie. It is kind of fun looking at all the animation screens. The movie is on track so it should still be out in December.

How is your mom doing? I know we say so much in email but I figured I wanted to write like I used to. I miss you so much. Sorry that I have been so busy lately.

That is cool that you are teaching piano now. Hey, kind of like your name! Well, hold on, someone is at the door. Let me see who it is.....

I left the letter in mid-sentence as I went to go answer the door. Standing at my doorstep was Lyric. "Hey!" I pulled her close in a tight bear hug. "I was just writing you. What are you doing here?"

"Well, I haven't seen you in so long. I just had to see you you know what I mean?" She asked me. And I knew exactly what she meant.

She followed me inside. Sam was barking and wagging his tail happily at my company. "Oh, Sam is so cute!" She squealed, petting him.

"Hey, now, you are supposed to say that about me, not him!"

"Well, he is the one with puppy dog eyes," she laughed. I liked the fact she was being gentle around his blind eye, making sure she did not go near it.

"How is your mom?"

"She is much better. Doctors say she is in remission."

"That's great."

"Yeah. We still have to watch her colitis to make sure she doesn't need a blood transfusion but she is getting stronger everyday. Stacey is still working on that cure."

"Oh, that reminds me." I held up my new Sleuthing Sam book. It was called *Sleuthing Sam Gets Help From The Twins*. "I had actually made Stacey and Stella characters in it. I had dedicated it to them."

"Oh, wow, they are going to be absolutely thrilled."

"Also, as promised." I gave her a copy of *Lyric's Lilacs* and she smiled brightly.

"Huntley?"

"Yes, Lyric?"

"Um, I am waiting on you to kiss me." She sighed. It was rather cute. I walked over to her and did as requested. It was amazing as always. I could have kissed her for hours but spending time with her was all I ever needed and talking to her. "Lyric, I love you."

"I love you, too, Huntley."

I felt like I had found my soulmate. She was really something. My mom would be over later and I could introduce them. "How long are you here?" I asked her.

"Well, believe it or not, my dad took our whole family here on a trip for a few days. He rented one of those resorts and wanted to surprise us with a trip to Disney. I know you are a couple hours away from there but they gave me permission to come see you. So just a few hours but I had to see you."

"I know what you mean. I don't have to work on the movie tomorrow so I can hang out at Disney with you then. Would that be okay?" I asked her.

"Absolutely, if you don't mind hanging out with the twins."

"Of course not. I will show them my new book," I smiled.

"They will love it. You want to go for a walk? I would love for you to show me around."

"Sure, we can walk Sam. It is pretty cool that you surprised me just like I surprised you."

"Not quite! You aren't in your bathrobe." Lyric laughed.

"You will never let me live that down."

"Nope, I won't."

"I see how you are," I teased her. As I was getting Sam's leash ready, I noticed Lyric looking at my piano.

"Oh, before we walk Sam, you got to let me hear you play." I told Lyric.

She nodded. She didn't think of protesting as her eyes lit up as she started tinkering with the keys. "I wrote this for my mom. I hope you like it."

She softly sung with the melody.

Butterfly wishes coming true
I wished with all my might
to comfort you
I was hoping and praying
you'd be okay
But I knew my heart was breaking
as the clouds turned gray
My spirit was broken
beyond repair
But God mended me
with His loving care
He will get His by

his wonderful grace
I know this every time
I look upon your face
I love you, Mom, just remember
Hold onto Jesus
He is everything
We will get past December
as the bluebird sings

"Wow, Lyric, that was really pretty." I was amazed at how talented Lyric was. The piano playing was so pretty and her voice so melodic.

"Thank you. Are you ready to walk Sam?"

"Yep, I am." And so we headed out the door and I loved that I got to spend time with my favorite girl (besides my mom) and my good ole faithful dog. God knew I needed them both. And the way she smiled at me, I knew she needed me.

The End!

135

Diary Devotional Books:
Life Hurts, God Heals
Beyond Grief, God's Relief

Quests of Enchantment Series:
A Mystical Journey
The Enchanted Entrance

Kaitiebug the Ladybug
Poetic Dreams

Info About The Cancer Ribbon

There are many different colors that make up cancer awareness ribbons. These ribbons may represent more than one cause.

The idea started with Charlotte Hayley, who handed out peach colored ribbons to raise awareness. She was a breast cancer survivor herself. Alexandra Penney loved the idea and wanted to feature it in her magazine but Hayley rejected it fearing it was too commercialized. So Penny who wanted to honor her founder of the magazine she worked for, who died of breast cancer, chose pink. Working with another breast cancer survivor, Evelyn Lauder, she was able to give them out at makeup counters.

Pink is the most recognized color so that is why I chose that color for the front of the book. I never mention what kind of cancer Lyric's mom has but pink is most commonly associated with breast cancer. And October is breast cancer awareness month so it felt right to publish it then.

All cancers can be represented by a light purple. My mom had cervical cancer which is teal and white. Lung cancer is white. My granddaddy had leukemia, which is orange. My grandmother died from bone cancer, which is yellow. My high school best friend passed away from appendix cancer, which is amber.

No matter what color, the main cause is for us to be aware. It hurts no matter how pretty the color is that represents the cancer that affected our lives. That turned our world upside down. Do what Lyric did. Talk to someone, no matter what. It is important. If you are the one suffering from cancer, or if you are the one being the caregiver. It is hard. I have been there I know.

The emails in this book are real and so if you do choose to write, I will respond. It feels like my characters are very much alive and I feel like if you need to talk to them, no matter, what you are going through, it helps to talk I know.

But also, pray to God. Jesus will hold your hand and guide your steps along the way. He loves you and cares for you.

My mom actually did say Never Let Go Of Jesus and I will never do that. I love Him like He loves us. My mom was cancer free when she died, but her colitis eventually made her lose too much blood.

But she, even it was just for a year was a cancer survivor. And I was so grateful I had been there for her. I hope you liked my story and that it helps you.

For info about Hayley and Penney
and cancer ribbon colors:
Source: www.wikipedia.org